SKYLAND
A Diary

Andrew Durbin

NIGHTBOAT BOOKS
NEW YORK

ISBN: 978-1-64362-027-5

Cover art: Alex Katz, *Sunrise*, 2019, oil on linen
Courtesy the artist and Gavin Brown's
enterprise, New York/Rome
© Alex Katz / VAGA at Artists Rights Society
(ARS), NY

Design and typesetting by Brian Hochberger
Text set in Futura and Caslon 540

Cataloging-in-publication data is available
from the Library of Congress

Nightboat Books
New York
www.nightboat.org

For Julien Archer and Shiv Kotecha

AUGUST 13

I woke to Julien pressed against my bedroom wall, sunlight cottoning the curtains above our heads, the damp remains of a joint lying in a tin dish on the desk, my pillow fallen behind the headboard, two unmatched pairs of socks scattered at the base of the bed, wrinkled shorts piled on the floor.

There will be a solar eclipse in a week and the anticipation of change has absorbed all of New York. Where best to see it, whether the clearest view will be in Pennsylvania or farther west—Ohio, Kentucky, even Missouri, any place out from the shadow of skyscrapers. Someone tells me an eclipse like this happens only once in a lifetime, so take care not to miss it. Others are convinced it portends the advent of a new world. Specially-made viewing glasses are now difficult to find. But I won't be in the city to see it.

I am meeting my friend Shiv in Athens tomorrow, where we will catch a boat to Patmos, a small, rocky island off the Turkish coast. He's rented us an apartment—part of a cheap

3

hotel complex he found through a Greek bookings site—for a week. The rooms, which aren't pictured, are said to be "cozie," with single beds, a shared kitchen and bathroom. Views of the sea aren't available at our price range; instead, the agent reserved us rooms that open to the ground-floor courtyard, with access to a communal balcony overlooking the bay. Shiv has spent the better part of a year in Athens attempting to finish his dissertation but, in the great tradition of advanced education, he's found himself endlessly distracted by wine and boys and, now, an island in the East Aegean.

We agreed to spend August 21st at the Cave of the Apocalypse, where we won't see the eclipse but hope the holy site will rival it in its own mysteries. I imagine palming the cubby-hole where John the Divine received his vision of the end-times, the stone soft and warm from the countless hands who have touched it before me. In emails, Shiv and I joke about the ways our pilgrimage might make believers of us, though we aren't Christians—nor plan to be. "Believers in what?" I wrote. We wonder if the coincidence of our visit, just as the sun disappears behind the moon over the United States, will suddenly, somehow, shock us into a conversion. Or, if not a conversion exactly, then the feeling of some inner potential becoming real and part of our lives, as it had for hundreds of thousands of pilgrims. "Not a chance," Shiv wrote.

I imagine ascending a narrow path up the island's rocky landscape, winding through gnarled trees, and ending at a vertical slit in the side of a mountain, where a homely Orthodox priest kneels before a gilded altar, chanting prayers. Beside him, the small vent where John lay his dreamy head.

I had hardly slept because of the joint. After finishing it, Julien and I had bad sex. He mostly wanted to talk in the dark, his bony shoulders touching mine, rather than do anything involving our cocks. I tried for more, but it went nowhere. Our mouths were too dry. Julien was sleepy. We were always clumsy with each other's bodies and could usually only come after a long slow effort, full of pauses to smoke or change the music on my laptop. Sometimes, we never made it that far. We would cuddle while watching YouTube or else sit up and talk about our families. He grew up in Virginia before coming to New York to make clothes for a theater costumier in Chelsea. His accent had faded in the years since he moved here, with only a soft twang present in the vowels after a few glasses of wine or whisky. I felt incomplete as he dozed off in my arms. Later, he drifted toward the wall as morning arrived.

I kept thinking about my transatlantic flight and the three-hour layover in Frankfurt, bad airport food—sausages and meaty sandwiches—and large, high-definition screens informing travelers of great deals and destinations. Greece, too, played on my mind. The buoyant sea. The grove of olive trees surrounding the Parthenon in Athens. Grilled sardines at the restaurants near Monastiraki Station. Shiv's apartment isn't far from the Archaeological Museum, on a slope that leads to a neighborhood called Exarchia, where anarchists organize against the government. His place has several rooms, including one for a live-in maid (there hasn't been a live-in maid in years), and a plant-filled terrace from which he could see the smoke from a smoldering university recently fire-bombed during a student-led riot. "You'd love it," he wrote over email. Marble floors, tiled walls. It belonged to the family of a graduate student at NYU who returned to the States, a boy Shiv met at a gay bar near Kerameikos.

In the early light, the wall glowed brightly with Julien pressed against it. I counted the blemishes on his shoulders: twenty or so were constellated across the tense muscles of his upper back, each small and pretty. He had spent the afternoon worrying about Hank, his middle brother, almost to the point of making himself sick. White nationalists were rallying for two days over the removal of a Confederate monument in Charlottesville and Hank, who lives in D.C. and works for a newspaper, went to photograph them. When a neo-Nazi driver ploughed into a group of counter-protesters, Hank's phone slipped from his hand in the scramble to get clear of the car, and its screen shattered. Nobody could reach him for hours, as footage of the killing of one protester, Heather Heyer, flooded our feeds. Finally, a friend lent Hank a phone and he called his mom, who called Julien, who came to my place to forget about what was happening down south. I hugged him and rolled a joint—cheap weed saved from his last visit. He sat in the window and watched me pack.

My spending a week on a remote island struck Julien as an excessive luxury, even if the rooms had only cost us a few hundred dollars. But this was more than a holiday with an old friend.

"I'm looking for a painting and I think it might take a while to find it," I said. "It's supposed to be on Patmos."

"What painting?"

"It's a portrait of the French writer and photographer I told you about, Hervé Guibert."

"Right," Julien said. "That guy."

That guy was the reason Shiv and I had chosen Patmos over any other island: I hoped the picture, which was only rumored to exist among those who follow Guibert's work closely, might convey something about its subject I hadn't yet gleaned from his autobiographical novels and photographs. Since I first encountered his work a few years ago, Guibert had become an obsession of mine, a constant presence in my reading life. Now, I told Julien, I might finally want to write about him. Not exactly a direct biography; rather, a sort of literary map of his personality, made using the memoirs—and paintings—of his lovers and friends. Thierry Jouno, his long-time partner. Michel Foucault, his famous friend and mentor. Christine Seemuller, Thierry's wife. And Yannis Tsarouchis, the Greek artist whose painting of Guibert is said to be on Patmos. Most of the people who were close to him are now dead, but they left behind enough artifacts from which the map might be constructed.

Guibert died in 1991, after living for a few years with AIDS. I told Julien about his struggle with the illness because that's what most readers learn when they first discover his books. I began there too with his late autobiographical novel, *To the Friend Who Did Not Save My Life*. Published the year before his death, the book is the opening of an informal cycle of works about Guibert's attempts—and ultimate failure—to secure life-extending medications that were spartanly distributed to men and women living with the disease at the time. The book was hugely successful in Paris, though less so in the English-speaking world. In another late work, *The Man in the Red Hat*, written shortly before he died and published posthumously, Guibert—now an art collector after finding himself flush with cash from the royalties of *To the Friend* and its sequel, *The Compassion Protocol*—goes to Greece to have his portrait done by Tsarouchis, or so he claims. Guibert was not always truthful, even in his most explicitly autobiographical fiction, which is replete with curious deaths, resurrections, and dreamt-up trips to war-torn countries in a world destroyed by disease. The difference between imagination and reality didn't carry much weight for him.

No one has seen the painting of Guibert by Tsarouchis, as far as I can tell. It might not even exist.

"I've been trying to track it down for months," I told Julien. "Now all signs point to Patmos."

"Why are you looking for it?"

"I want to see his face."

I've seen his gloomy eyes and shock of curly hair in plenty of self-portraits, but not as someone else had seen him, someone outside of the story he spent his life constructing. In his own pictures, he and his friends are preserved perfectly in their handsome youth. Yet, the photographs don't seem to capture the way he might have really lived, the expressions he made, the way he set his mouth. The sweat, and the smell of his skin. Painting can't quite express these qualities of his physical presence either but, still, I wanted to know what another person had made of Guibert when he was patient enough to sit for a portrait. To sit for someone else's hand.

Tsarouchis was an old man when Guibert met him in the mid-1980s, if he met him at all. His early-20th-century paintings of sailors—sailors with butterfly wings, sailors standing or bathing together, sailors dreaming of other sailors—drew on gay tropes that would become more popular after the Second World War. Following his return from Paris, where he had lived in exile during Georgios Papadopoulos's dictatorship of the late 1960s and early 1970s, Tsarouchis moved with his wife to the mountains of Corfu, Guibert reports, and became something of a national treasure—beyond questioning by the conservative art scene as to why he painted so many soldiers in jock straps.

Julien thinks my trip will be a wasteful, romantic exercise, but I've never staked my research on the promise of assured answers. Something always shoots up, seemingly out of nowhere, whenever I go looking for a stray bit of history. This isn't quite the grand, unfurling cliché of travel—"what matters is the journey and not the destination"—since all I want is a destination, an end point. No cheap Norwegian Air flight matters more than its arrival city. I'm not sure I need to find exactly what I'm looking for. A small desert island in a distant sea, a painting, a face.

Guibert dissected his own life, from childhood to death, with eerie confidence and remove. This is most true of his books: beginning with *To the Friend*, continuing in *The Compassion Protocol* and concluding with the posthumous novels *The Man in the Red Hat*, *My Valet and Me*, and *Paradise*. He recorded everything in near-humiliating detail. The failures of parents, the sadness of children. Defecation, fucking, not fucking, friendship, addiction, desire, disease, and death. Guibert has died so many times in literature—he dies or nearly dies, in some manner, in each of those late novels, as well as in the posthumous diary *Cytomegalovirus*—that I feel as if I carry his slim corpse with me. Dead in his fiction; dead at the end of his collected journals, *The Mausoleum of Lovers*; dead in Mathieu Lindon's memoir of his friendships with Foucault and Guibert, *Learning What Love Means*. Dead at thirty-six.

No one knows what Tsarouchis's painting looks like because Guibert tells the reader that he lost the pages describing it and he refuses to re-write them. Instead, I invent his face in the Greek painter's hands: thin, aquiline features arranged under matted hair (the curls gone with the virus's inexorable progress), all of it rendered thickly in oil paint. His expression is self-serious and mannered. Despite the revelatory character of his writing, his persistent urge to say too much too often, I imagine he tries to conceal from Tsarouchis the nevertheless perceptible fear that he is not so brave as his writing suggests. "You are wrong," the painting might retort. I could be wrong.

I've visited Athens only once before—after a long residency in Belgium, where I finished my first novel, *MacArthur Park*. At the time, a major retrospective of Tsarouchis's work was on view at the Benaki Museum. I had never seen his paintings of sailors undressing in baths and plain country rooms, hustlers gussied with butterfly wings, or the ornate sets for the Athenian opera and Maria Callas; until then, I only knew him as a character in *The Man in the Red Hat*, one who appears briefly toward the end of the story. Among hundreds of drawings and paintings, I had hoped to find the portrait of Guibert, but no one at the museum knew what I was talking about, or if the painting even existed.

I went to Paris and asked Christine Seemuller, who has overseen Guibert's estate since his death, if she knew where the painting might be, but she suspected it was fiction. I refused to believe her. It seemed too real in the novel: his depiction of the artist's studio and the agony of posing for as long as he did, even if the description of the painting itself is lost. "If it does exist," she told me over a glass of wine in a café near the Centre Pompidou, "then I have never seen it and I bet no one in Paris has either."

I wrote to administrators of art foundations and private collections, his ex-lovers, friends of friends, fellow novelists, galleries who had worked with either Guibert or Tsarouchis. Those who answered had no idea if the painting was extant, and most had never heard of it. A Tsarouchis dealer told me, "Yannis was prolific and gave so many works away. You never know. We hear these stories all the time. It might be kicking around somewhere. Probably in Greece."

Shiv said, "If you fly to Athens, I'm sure you'll find it. Greece is like that." I was unconvinced. Weeks later, he introduced me over email to Telemachos, who sits on the board of a Greek art foundation and knew Tsarouchis in the 1980s. A retired winery owner named Alekos had apparently purchased the painting years ago; Telemachos had seen it with his own eyes. It hangs in Alekos's summer house on Patmos, far from the Greek mainland, he told me. "He might be interested in selling it to you. He is old and no longer cares for these things." I didn't want to buy the portrait and couldn't have afforded it anyway. I just wanted to see Guibert's face.

I booked a flight, and then a Superfast ferry to Patmos. Shiv wanted to tag along—for the beaches.

"Extravagant," Julien said, pulling on his shirt.

AUGUST 14

At Piraeus, a fleet of cruise ship-sized ferries bobbed at the docks. They were larger than anything I had imagined—ten or more stories high, broad enough to carry hundreds of passengers. Not the medium-sized hydrofoils that operate in the English Channel or off the East Coast, between Long Island and mainland New York. They loomed over the port, which was in the midst of intensive renovation and construction after an influx of Chinese investment. Cranes dangled over the waterfront, with workers scurrying under them, between interconnecting scaffolding. I found Shiv at a café outside the train terminal, drinking fizzy espresso in the heat. A few other passengers stood nearby, under sweaty, plastic-walled cubicles next to the bus stop. The air was still and dry, even by the water. He was several pounds lighter after a year's diet of olives and cucumbers, leafy greens, fish—handsome as before, but fresh-faced. A new Shiv. Or newish. "You're too skinny." I meant, *Aren't you* hot? Meaning, *I've missed you*. He said, "I never want to leave." We were a few hours early; the boat wasn't set to depart until closer to dinner.

We went into town for lunch: baked cheese and fish, Greek salad, cold Orangina. I told Shiv New York hadn't changed, and I could tell he didn't quite miss it. His cat was fine without him; the poets were still reading the same poems; most of our favorite restaurants hadn't closed, though many were on the verge of doing so. He shrugged at the gossip, that some writers we knew had finally moved elsewhere—to Los Angeles and Oakland and Philadelphia—and that others had chosen to stay, even after threatening for years to leave. "I'm not ready to go back, but I'm sure I'll be fine once I'm home." You wouldn't know it from his voice, which sounded with a note of disappointment at the word "home." Writing his dissertation had gone slowly, he explained, without saying why. Probably because he had spent most of the year tinkering with poems and drinking wine in cafés. He showed me a few new ones, then waited to hear what I thought. They were good, as good as anything he'd written. They were about fucking his roommate in Brooklyn, not that he ever had. "Years of mistaking / friendship," he read aloud from a document on his phone:

> ...for romance
> and asking each other
>
> over and over again
> not for each other
>
> but for each other's
> reassurance of who they
>
> are to the other...

I nodded, "I like it."

By dusk, the boat was full. Hundreds of passengers, mostly Greeks and Western Europeans, arrived in the hour before we disembarked, loaded their suitcases into the ship's hull, where supply trucks were parked stern to prow. Most crowded onto the top decks and waved to friends and family and the other ships as we left Piraeus. Once the ferry cleared the port, some passengers decamped to their private rooms or to the cafés on the bottom decks, or else sat on the roof with bottles of wine between their thighs, talking excitedly in Greek and German and French and some English. Clouds of cigarette smoke wafted among them, then quickly dissipated in the whoosh of sea air. We would make several stops throughout the night, the captain announced, along the Dodecanese chain of islands, with Patmos toward the end, around early morning. Shiv said, "It's not popular like it once was, I've heard. But that might make it interesting." I scanned the crowd for people our age, but I could only find families of young children or teenagers, with a few middle-aged couples mixed among them. The islands on our line weren't major gay destinations, like Mykonos. The late-summer crowds of handsome young American and British tourists vacationed elsewhere, in the Cyclades. Shiv didn't mind. He liked the idea of a holiday on the periphery. So did I.

We ate fried fish, potatoes, a slice of cake in the cafeteria. Warm sparkling water and retsina, since the ship's refrigeration had fritzed shortly after we went to sea. The wine bottle's label was lime green and showed the silhouette of a man with a giant door key sticking out of his belly. "The barrels are sealed with pine sap, which explains the flavor," Shiv said. "Do you like it?"

"Yes," I gulped. Bitter, almost sour, it tasted like pine needles, sure. Shiv loved everything about Greece, even its bad wine. I sipped from my glass again. "I like it." I'd learn to love it.

The Aegean turned choppier the farther we listed from the coastline, and we had to hold our plates to keep them from sliding off the table. Shiv said, "I can't tell if the ocean seems worse because I'm drunk." With that, his plate of fish and potatoes slipped from his hand and spilled across the carpet.

We spent the rest of the night outside, on reclining chairs arranged around an empty pool on the top deck. Most passengers not in their rooms slept in the carpeted stair-well or else lounged on benches in the caf-eteria, reading magazines and staring at their phones. Service was intermittent; texts from friends came through in sporadic bursts, alongside notifications from *The New York Times* about things President Trump had said and done since Charlottesville. I watched a puddle climb the curve of the pool basin as the boat tilted to the left, then to the right, then to the left again. I wasn't sick yet, but I thought I might be if we didn't stabilize soon. Shiv whispered to himself, "I hate this." The puddle bubbled with mud. A few couples, teenagers, some families kept awake, either drinking, smoking, talking by the railing, unbothered by the violent back-and-forth of the waves. When we hung left, they held steady and whispered as if nothing was hap-pening. Nothing *was* happening. We seemed to have slipped out of time, along some vector of perpetual night, into—into what, I didn't know. Or where. The idea of any place other than the boat had become faint in the few hours since we'd boarded. Like we were going nowhere and yet moving all the same, the Aegean churning furiously below. The whole world dropped away, into the dark, under a cloudy and starless sky. A couple reclined on chairs across the pool from us, their two sons sitting on their laps. The boys were close in age, sixteen or seventeen, a little old to be lying on their parents, but then the intimacy between families in Europe was unfamiliar to me. One of the boys was older, with long, curly hair and acne-scarred cheeks. His brother's face, smaller and rounder, was covered by a thick layer of zinc lotion, his identifying features reduced to two huge blue eyes and flaking lips. The oldest tossed two empty beer bottles into the air and started to juggle. Not to be outdone, the younger boy grabbed his dozing father by the chin and kissed him on the lips. They burst into laughter.

"What's our plan for Patmos?"

Shiv lowered his voice, "We go to the beach, we drink retsina. I'd like to meet someone cute!"

"Why are you whispering?"

Near midnight, the clouds cleared, and the ferry steadied on calmer ocean. Shiv opened a star-gazing app and held it to the sky. It named the planets and constellated the stars into the shapes of animals and gods. Aquila, Cygnus, and Lyra. Saturn, my ruling planet. Mercury. We slurred through the names together, then fell silent as a cool wind blew across the deck. Another bottle of retsina.

"Any news on that painting?" he asked.

"No, not really. I asked Alekos to put me in touch with the guy on Patmos, but I haven't heard back yet. Seems like a fluke, anyway."

"That's everything out here. You hear about someone you should meet, and the next thing you know, they're sitting across from you at a café. It's a small country. You'll find him."

I appreciated his confidence but, as we cruised toward what seemed like the end of the world, or at least the end of *a* world, the plan to meet Alekos and see his portrait of Guibert felt less plausible than it had in New York. Last week, the distance between

Brooklyn and Patmos had allowed me to imagine all sorts of possibilities for the search. Every room in every house might contain some important totem—not only the painting but other resonant objects of mystic purpose.

Now that I was almost there, I wondered if I had flown to Greece in haste. Sailing to the apartment of a stranger, someone I only knew through a third party, and who, crazily, I hadn't spoken to directly or met, made no sense. Still, the rush of coming to the island without firmer plans was thrilling. The chance that, out of thin air, I might find what I was looking for, since my research had so far proven fruitless. As I saw it, I'd had no choice but to fly. I just wasn't so sure I knew what I was doing.

I first discovered Guibert by chance. An editor sent me a PDF of his photographs in the hope that I might write about them for his magazine. I asked Twitter where to start with the novels, and a stranger—a professor at a small college in Rhode Island whose name I've forgotten—suggested *To the Friend*

Who Did Not Save My Life. He mailed me an English edition with a faded, purplish hard-back cover. In the novel's first paragraph, Guibert declares that he has contracted AIDS, which would normally be a death sentence, but "by an extraordinary stroke of luck," he will become "one of the first people on earth to survive this deadly malady." I inhaled *To the Friend*, then re-read it while waiting for his other books to arrive in the mail, all of them translated in the early 1990s and now out of print. There was the novel about his parents, the short book on going blind. Experiments in autobiography and in making things up. I discovered in Guibert a kindred spirit, one who had passed away, into literary history, when I was a child and he was in his thirties. I wasn't nearly as hand-some, or accomplished, or even as sexually adventurous; I hadn't made my romances and friendships into the kind of sustaining art that he had, but I wanted to, badly, and I recognized in him some close proximate of my own desire to mix real life and fiction. I didn't have a handle on it. Still don't. But his sentences, even the sloppiest, were my ideal sentences. Or some version of them.

I was also infatuated with Guibert's lover, Thierry, and their love was, for a long time, my ideal love. In the novels, he's Jules, and not nearly as vivid as he is in Guibert's photographs of him. A distance separates them, at least in translation, intensified by the fact that Guibert changed his name, as if their attraction to one another couldn't find its way into language, only photographs. And just barely. In one, Thierry sits with a book in his lap, his hair wet from a bath or swimming in the sea. Guibert holds the camera above him so that his lover's bangs conceal his eyes. I imagine their life then: they were at the beach on Elba together, in a cheap hotel familiar to them from years of visiting the island. They had just showered, fucked in the summer darkness afterwards, on the flimsy cot where Thierry now sits, though they had agreed earlier in the year to stop sleeping together since intimacy only jolted awake the dormant, sometimes painful, history between

them. Everything in their shared life is provisional now, worked out in careful argu-
ments over the years, on short holidays and
during late nights at cafés in Paris. Thierry
eventually leaves Guibert for Christine, who
later marries Guibert, after he decides he
wants to bequeath his newfound wealth from
writing to Christine and Thierry's children,
rather than to his own family. Thierry dies
from AIDS first; Guibert knows he won't live
much longer himself and dies shortly there-
after. The photograph doesn't know any of
this, but it senses it all the same.

When I met Christine in Paris, I asked
her what had attracted the two men to one
another. She hated the question. It was the
worst question anyone had ever put to her
about Guibert and her late husband. She said,
"How can you ask this? How can I tell you
how it was? How could I know?" She finished
her wine and described their relationship by
quoting Michel de Montaigne in French,
refusing to translate, "Parce que c'était lui,
parce que c'était moi."

The parents left the two teenaged boys to themselves. They played quietly at first but after we swiped the crest of another wave their voices steadily increased. They flapped their arms and pretended to fly in circles around the pool, shouting in German until they fell back on their chairs in fits of laughter. Shiv tried to say something to me, but I was too distracted—and too drunk—to follow. When he raised his voice, they zeroed their attention on us. The youngest, with the zinc-covered face, stared ahead, his eyes darting between Shiv and me. His head hung like a bright, swiveling lamp on his thin neck. He slapped his knees and leaned forward, shouting, "Hey, hey!" We ignored him. He repeated himself, louder, "Hey." "Hey." "Hey." "Hey." "HEY!" I turned. The oldest leaped onto the chair and flashed his hard-on at us, which the younger boy tugged a few times before his brother yanked up his shorts and sat down. The outline of his penis pressed through the plasticky material, along his thigh. He touched it again, without breaking eye contact with me. Or Shiv. They wanted our attention and now held it nervously, unsure of what to do. It would end in a split second but, before that, the split devoured us. I forgot about the motion of the waves or Shiv beside me. I wanted to turn away or leave but couldn't move. The air, whipping across the deck, silenced everything but my heartbeat until the loudspeaker crackled with the announcement, in Greek and English, that we were arriving at the next island. The moment ended, spit us out, into the night. The boy closed his legs, shrugged his shoulders, and left with his brother.

AUGUST 15

We arrived at Skala, the island's only port, around four in the morning, the too-sweet taste of pine coating our mouths, bellies stuffed with cheap fish pies from the ferry's late-night canteen. The hotel owner told us ahead of time that his yaya would hide the keys under a painted stone in the stairwell between our two rooms. On the narrow, irregular pathways that divided the hotel's apartments, clutches of pink flowers hung among vines and succulents, the flora of an arid island, an exile island, where the Devil was once turned to rock and Saint John cast him into the sea.

Shiv stumbled down a stair that led to a small courtyard canopied with hanging laundry, into a nest of sleeping kittens. They squeaked and scrambled into the bushes, five or so white and grey balls of fur. I suggested we jump into the bay to cure ourselves of the booze and, possibly, prevent a hangover before going to bed. He nodded. His eyes were bloodshot and partly closed. I hadn't slept in what felt like days.

We stood in our underwear and watched the ferry pull away. Smooth rocks rolled gently under my feet as the boat's rudder churned the water in the bay. It was destined for Leros or Kos; I couldn't remember which island had been announced as we disembarked. Solid ground took getting used to again.

Nobody had warned us how far the island was from Piraeus. Eight hours by boat, as we finished bottle after bottle of retsina, felt like nearly a lifetime at sea, especially under the haze of jet lag. When Patmos had finally appeared on the horizon, we could only make out two cleaved points of light against the starry backdrop: one for the ancient town on the mountain top, Chora, and another for Skala. Between the two, the Cave hid among darkened trees. Only a nip of land.

From the hill where our apartment stood, we could see the dim outline of Lipsi: the small island nearest Patmos, where the devout worship Christ as the lotus flower. None of the larger boats ever went there, Shiv learned in his research, and beyond Lipsi lay the west coast of Turkey, where refugees lingered by the seaside, waiting for safe crossing to Samos—an island of camps.

AUGUST 16

Guibert's final novel, *Paradise*, begins on an island in the South Pacific, after his lover, Jayne, dies on a reef while swimming in heavy surf. He dwells, in the opening pages, on her disfiguring wounds, shocked by the mindless violence of the sea; he cannot overcome the horror of seeing her destroyed genitals in the city's makeshift morgue, and visions of her mangled body plague his dreams and waking thoughts. Local police suspect foul play— their unmarked cars circle Guibert's hotel. But her absence, and the trouble it produces, is brief. Jayne returns to the story shortly after her death, her resurrection unacknowledged and unexplained.

Guibert used death and illness to dissolve and restructure his characters into different versions of themselves through a jerry-rigged immortality. Lovers seldom die, even when they do. *Crazy for Vincent* opens with the demise of the titular boyfriend though he resurrects almost immediately when the narrative reverses. Death's transformative potential obsessed Guibert early in his writing life.

In the late 1970s, he wrote what might be read as an early treatment for *Paradise* in his diary:

It's death that drives me (that would be the end of the book).

Saturday evening. Wine and solitude put me in one of those states: I write my obituary.

(Africa.)

In *Paradise*, Jayne and Guibert traverse islands along the equator, arriving finally at an abandoned nightclub in Ségou, Mali, where a mysterious, unnamed disease slowly wastes them. Flies nick their flesh. Food runs low. They lounge in their squatters' quarters, dying and yet deathless: paranoid white folk tended by children who run off with what little money they have left after their travels. Civil war surrounds the club, but the effects of conflict are muted, only noticeable in the distant sound of gunfire. Guibert slips into a state of limbic paralysis, "unable to remember anything

44

[…] no longer able to speak, nor move my left arm." Who will save him when Jayne is gone, and where will he go? The book sputters and pops, growing more confusing as the confusions of the disease—and the war—take hold.

Paradise was the result of a hallucinatory episode near the end of Guibert's life, when he collapsed in the street from fever. The novel ends in a wholly different reality, far from its original narrative, with its author lying in a hospital bed in Paris. He reports:

> I am someone with a double life, sometimes a writer, at other times nothing; I'd liked to be a triple, quadruple personality, a dancer, a gangster, a tightrope walker, a painter, a skier. I'd like to have a delta plane and throw myself into the void, speed like a thunderbolt down pistes whose snow would be heroin. I have made myself the victim of a schizophrenic device [for] creating dual personalities.

Shortly before writing *Paradise*, Guibert shot *Modesty or Shame*, a 62-minute documentary about the cruel routine of his last days. He is cared for by a nurse whose face we don't see; he sinks into a sofa chair, surrounded by books, his hand covering his eyes; he goes to Elba, where eventually his ashes will be dispersed by friends.

An island: "(that would be the end of the book)."

It was our first full day on Patmos after spending the day before recovering from jet lag in bed. Early morning to late afternoon, sun. Retsina for breakfast, with cut cucumbers and Kalamata olives. The kittens warmed themselves on the porch, purring softly when we invited them to sit in our laps. They accepted Shiv's apology after his stumble on our first night.

"What should we do?" he asked. A small gray thing stretched across his lap.

There is only the beach "to do" on the island, so we went to the nearest, about a half mile from our hotel. We sat on the shore under a shady tree and read while Turkish millionaires dined on their yachts anchored in the bay.

In the evening, we learned from fellow residents at the hotel that there is almost no internet access on the island, except at a few cafés in Skala and Chora. My email with Alekos's address wouldn't load. How could I have forgotten to write it down before we left Athens? There must be a dozen men with his name here and I had no way of finding him. I remembered that he lived in Chora, near a bar called Astivi, popular with tourists, including David Bowie, who used to stay at a friend's house on Patmos decades ago. Alekos "has a gin and tonic at sunset every evening," Telemachos told me. I remembered that.

We ate dinner on the communal porch overlooking the bay. A salad of cucumber, feta, and different olives I bought from a roadside stand not far from us. The olives, green and black and blue-gray, were ladled from huge vats into a plastic sack—fermented, the stall's owner explained, using a mix of spices and salts from a thousand-year-old recipe.

Shiv said, "We'll find Alekos soon. There's no rush. Nobody's going anywhere."

AUGUST 17

We started at the nearest beach again, haven't yet caught its name, stared at the citadel in Chora, high above us. Will the apocalypse begin here or elsewhere? Yesterday, a taxi driver who shuttled us across the island to an inlet known for the smoothness of its colored stones said "the law" forbade nudity in view of the citadel. "No naked. It's the law." The citadel can be seen from almost anywhere on the island, so we stayed in our swimsuits wherever we went.

You can easily float on the surface of the Aegean. I let the waves carry me toward open water, where the view to the bottom became murky. In the distance, past yachts and sailboats, Lipsi rippled under blinding blue. "We should go," Shiv said, after pointing it out while we arranged our towels. "There are day ferries." A lump of rock and sand like any other island here, but I agreed with him that its devotion to the lotus flower was suggestive; we both wanted to see the tile steps that lead up to the church, which are apparently inlaid with the symbol.

Adrift, I tried to imagine the ways I would describe the color of the light and landscape on Patmos. Mornings and afternoons have so far offered mute shades of yellow and blue. Only in the evening, at sunset, does another spectrum, softly pink with purple filigree, gauze the island. The seabed is patchy with black stones and forests of unfamiliar plants. On the other side of the island, one beach is purportedly sandy, the water clear, but near Skala, it is difficult to see very far down. When my feet touch the floor, gooey pebbles lodge between my toes. Cliffs of orange and white stone flocked with wild flowers and scratchy grass droop over thundering waves. Uninhabitable islands jut out in the distance sometimes with a few trees clinging to their sides.

I watched Shiv talk to men on the shore. He and I spent the morning staring at them as they loped to the water, fiddled with a portable radio, napped under a gnarled tree, hoping they might take an interest in us. They didn't. Instead they admired their own bodies and argued in French. Shiv swore he had seen one on a cruising app during a fleeting moment of connection, a guy wearing a white polo hat—by far the cutest of the bunch. He recognized him by the tattoo of a dragon on his left shoulder. We speculated loudly enough about his profile for our voices to carry over to their picnic, but until Shiv mustered the courage to say hello, they pretended not to hear us and kept to themselves. The one Shiv had seen online was handsome, mid-forties, with a slight paunch and thick chest hair that swirled around his bright pink nipples. The dragon's tail swooped across his right bicep. Finally, as I drifted out to sea, Shiv stood up and walked over to their group. The man from the app handed him a glass and motioned to sit down.

Later, I swam to the shallows—

"We're going to go buy wine from a grocery up the road," Shiv said. "Do you want anything?"

"I don't think so."

—And then went back to the sea.

Half an hour passed without Shiv or retsina. I wondered if I should hail a cab to the next beach on my own—our plan had been to hop to a few, with lunch on the other side of the island—and meet him there, or else wait. We had promised to have fun, with or without the other, and I hoped he was having plenty on his own. I sat in the sand to dry off while the Frenchman's friends packed their things and left. Shiv must have gone to our hotel, I thought. I decided to walk to the taverna and see if they would call me a car.

A goat, which had been watching me swim from the shade of a fig tree, accompanied me to the restaurant, a bell clanging on its neck. Its slotted eyes widened when I asked whether it needed a ride. It stopped, cocked its head. "I'm kidding." We both smelled of dirt and sweat and salt.

Over the far hill, Shiv appeared as the cab arrived at a bend in the road. He and the Frenchman had not even passed the rocks near the farm a few yards away before they started fucking among the half-wild chickens. The grocery was closed for a lunch break by the time they reached it, and the Frenchman—Shiv had already forgotten his name, though he did get his number—had to meet his brothers for a jog to Chora. "How was it? It was wonderful," he said, with a smile.

The yaya speaks little English. She nods and says, "Yes," even when the answer is most certainly, "No."

"Is there a night market near us?"

"Yes." But we learned, later, there isn't.

"Can you tell us where?"

"No."

"Do you happen to know when the boat to Lipsi leaves?"

"Yes."

"What time?"

"Yes."

The lack of a shared language doesn't prevent us from understanding one another. She smiles when she answers our questions, pleased with how helpful she thinks she's been. I like her, even if she doesn't know what I'm saying. The whole island relies on glances and some inward sense of its custom. Outside of ordering lunch, words are fairly useless, especially in the afternoon heat, when everyone moves slowly, seeking only shade.

She gave me a handful of cooked fish to feed the cats on my way out this morning. "For cat," she said, nodding to the kittens playing at the bottom of the stair. She clapped when they ate from my hand.

Bougainvillea clings to the courtyard walls amid pale anemones. The air smells of herbs. At end of day, the light, hazy and full of dust, fades and falls to sea. You can see clear across the Aegean to the neighboring islands, almost as if your eyes were suddenly capable of magnifying. On Lipsi and Samos, trees and rocks come into sharp relief against the mountains; in the morning and afternoon they appear as only incomplete shapes dumped at the horizon line—islands of desert in the midst of water. Farther out, Turkey promises Asia and delivers. Shades of orange, red, yellow color the air until the surrounding islands blur again. As the sun sinks, mauve light seeps into the lower sky before fading to starry blue.

Each house here keeps a solar-powered water heater on its roof labeled, in English, "Skyland."

AUGUST 18

Guibert flies to Tsarouchis's home on Corfu, but the painter has made an unplanned trip. His wife, Gertrud, doesn't know when he will return—or where he has gone. It could be days, even weeks. Guibert is close to collapse, his lesions have turned to festering wounds. Gertrud sets up a guest room where he can rest. I wonder if she is familiar with AIDS, what it was doing to gay men and women around the world, if she suspects her husband might be at risk. Guibert never says. He sleeps for days and wakes, in the middle of the night, to the household dog nibbling at his lesions. He's too weak to stop her. She bears down on his chest and plunges her tongue into his throat, growing hungrier with each lick. Finally, he manages to throw her off, but the damage has been done; his sores are open and bleeding.

Guibert waits for more than Tsarouchis. There's also whatever else might follow the painter through the door when he returns from his trip, the thing the world is dragging into existence. An ending, or paradise. Guibert carries the anticipation of it within him every-where, the sensation of its ever-arriving.

In Greece, I am wracked by a sense of the ever-arriving event, person, painting. Indefinite, hulking, immaterial, cloudy, moody things, always skulking somewhere over some bit of rock. It's either time or history. A forged zone of irregularities, slipshod moments, over- or underspent hours. Teas, cakes, bread, wine, olives, fish, fries, wine again. Endless anticipation, as if Patmos is a waiting room and, soon, a boat will arrive at harbor to ferry me to the place where I'm sup-posed to be. It always comes as an unsettling premonition, like an ache before the onset of fever, my arms tense, my forehead sweaty and hot. What next.

Psili Ammos. Greek for "fine sand."

I drew forward into the sun after a bus ride to the end of the island. A donkey trudged past us, down a path that wound toward the ocean. It stopped to issue a misty snort with each precipitous drop. Shiv idled beneath a

62

fossilized tree. "Hurry up," he said. We were late for nothing.

"Why don't we get it over with?" I pointed to the city above us. "And go to Chora."

The citadel emanates the weird reliquary influence of an obsolete authority. I found myself looking over my shoulder whenever I walked through Skala, half expecting to glimpse shadowy figures spying on me from its ancient windows.

"The beach is so nice. Let's wait till the 21st. We'll go to the Cave and then to Chora. The painting isn't going anywhere."

He didn't take my search seriously, but I decided not to push it since he was right: Alekos would be there when we finally got to town. We'd climb the stairs and arrive at the restaurant's porch where he sips his regular gin and tonic. A few waiters, all in starched white collared shirts, slightly unshaven, handsome, decent enough at French and English, would show us to a table overlooking Patmos and the surrounding islands. A few other diners would be working through lamb and cold beer. All Greeks. Which one would he be? The graying man in white t-shirt and blue trousers, his face buried in the paper, a glass beside him with a green bottle of tonic on a laminated menu. "Alekos?"

Psili Ammos was full. We'd spent every day so far on other beaches, all mostly empty, wondering where everyone might be but, finally, we had made it to Psili Ammos—the last on our list, the first on everyone else's. Pretty boys played in the shallow bay, with their girlfriends. There were even some Americans throwing a Frisbee. Hearing English, or at least English from a native speaker, was jarring, more jarring than French or German. The sound of an unwelcome phone call from home, a reminder that soon we would have to get going, board the boat, and cruise back to the mainland.

A spot opened between families and a group of British boys with a radio playing the BBC. The President of the United States was angry. The United Kingdom still intended to leave

Europe. France's new leader was the same as the old French leaders. I tried to ignore the news, which would only make me think of home, and concentrate instead on the novel I had brought with me. The words on the page refused to stick in my mind as the voices on the radio debated a looming American trade war with China. Muddy plot. Nameless characters. I stood up and went to dunk my head in the waves.

Julien might ask later, "What did you do the whole time?"

I could show him these entries: "Stood around. Ate a little. Swam." Then add, "I missed you."

"But did you?" he'd ask, not quite believing I had thought about him at all.

On the beach, Shiv wondered how the water was. "The best," I said, though it was like the water elsewhere: warm and buoyant.

The British boys waded out. One's speedo had ridden up his ass and was dusted with sand, a scene as mesmerizing as any I had witnessed on Patmos so far. He adjusted the fabric around his right cheek—a taut square of muscle—as he tiptoed among the small waves. I stared dumbly. His arms were golden and blond. He and his friends nudged one another playfully while sinking into the clumpy sand before paddling out to the depths. I thought they were boys, but they were men only pretending to be boys for the sake of the holiday, or one another, or because the August heat had turned them mischievous and playful. When their heads broke against the choppy surface, I watched them shout things I couldn't hear over the sound of the other beachgoers, their mouths wide and full of bright teeth. I wanted to know what they were saying since those words possessed, in each secret and inside joke, an almost unbearable eroticism—or so I guessed. I was dizzy and panting under the sun.

"Have you heard from Julien?" Shiv asked.

"He texted me when we were on the boat."

"And…"

"And he sent me a selfie. I'll wait to respond until next week. I need a break."

"Do you actually like him?"

"Yes. But I don't know what to do with my feelings for him. If that makes sense."

Shiv left New York before he could meet Julien. I had shared with him a few pictures of us on bike rides or when we had lunch in the park on weekends, but these had only served to convey Julien's physical beauty, not his personality or why I was attracted to him—or was made so anxious by his grief during Charlottesville. I didn't know how to phrase what I felt for him. It was only sensible through touch and presence and feeling—not anything evincible in words. I liked him in a way that made me want to pretend he didn't exist when he wasn't in the room, since otherwise I risked thinking of nothing except Julien: *because it was him; because it was me*, as Montaigne wrote.

"For now, when I'm here, I don't want to fixate on our relationship, which, you're right, I don't understand. Otherwise, I'll be frantic about getting service all the time."

Shiv nodded. He picked up his phone to check for just that—enough bars for a few minutes online. The cruising apps weren't promising. The grid filled with men's torsos, seen only from the neck down, many of whom were on holiday with their wives and children, or so they said. Tonight, another Superfast ferry would arrive with new passengers, about whom we had tremendous unfounded hope. Otherwise, the most attractive men our phones picked up were on Mykonos, about 70 miles west of Patmos.

"He freaks you out."

"He doesn't freak me out."

"You don't like that he's so sensitive. The brother thing. Coming to your place. I know you."

"Not true. You've been gone a long time. How do you know I haven't changed?"

"I bet," Shiv said slowly, setting down his phone to pour wine from a bottle he'd stashed in his bag, "It *is* serious, and that's what bothers you so much. 'I'll think about nothing else?' He's already on your mind; you're just not saying so. He came to your place after he thought his brother might have been *killed*. That's something. You were the first person he thought of. You hate that."

I looked for the British boys in the water while listening to Shiv. Half of their group had scrambled up a jagged pyramid of rock and were waving to the others below. I dug my hands into the sand until they disappeared under a layer of its warm miniscule grains. It was as fine as the beach's name had promised.

When Julien had come to my apartment last week, I wasn't sure what to say. The afternoon felt unreal, as if I were living outside of it. His brother was alive, Heyer was dead, and the president had defended her killers. Even the name Charlottesville had taken on a dream-like quality, especially while I rushed to pack for my trip. Any comfort, which was the one thing I could give him, couldn't scale to the confusing nature of what had happened— what was happening—in Virginia. It was too big, too potent, too noisy. An ugly feeling was coursing through us, through all my friends, thickening our blood with its toxins. Not only grief, not only hate, not only rage, though it was composed in large part of those three core elements. It had no word, at least none I could recall. Some had already surrendered to it, and part of me, the part that hugged Julien in my door, but also wanted badly to push him away or else risk falling further into the unnamed feeling without knowing how it might end, wanted nothing more than to surrender to it, too. "I'm upset but grateful Hank wasn't hurt," he had said, as I showed him into my apartment.

"Did you know anyone else there?"

"I did."

"Do you want another hit of the joint?"

"Yeah."

"How do you feel?"

"Like everyone else does."

"So, shitty."

"Yeah, shitty."

Shiv waited for me to admit he was right. "You're right," I said. "I'll text him later. I'm sure he wants to know how it's going." I added, "If we found the painting yet."

Before lunch, Shiv swam to an isthmus at the edge of the bay. He promised to be quick: he only wanted to see what was on the other side. Probably more rock, a stray goat. A waiter in Skala said goats outnumbered people here two to one. After reaching it, his head bobbing against the surf, Shiv vanished. Five minutes, ten, fifteen passed. I scouted for him down by the water. The waves were rougher today but calling a rescue operation felt premature—he had grown up on the coast of California, had swum his whole life, maybe even competitively, though I couldn't remember whether that was true or if I had made it up to calm my nerves. (I had made it up.) Why worry? Thirty or more people were swimming, some as far out as the isthmus. I returned to our towels to read. Kids rushed the birds pecking for bits of fried fish left by the family sitting next to us. Radios and ocean and tourists, all roaring. I stood up, brushed the sand from my clothes and bag, looked for Shiv again, but he hadn't come back into view. My phone was dead, I had no way of knowing how long he had been gone. Twenty minutes? No more than thirty. The British boys were playing nearby, and I assumed they would have seen him had anything gone wrong. Or could he have been pulled down by a riptide, dragged into some underwater cave, part of a vast complex deep below the ocean floor? I imagined him struggling against the current or smashed on the rocks, his body cut by some razor-sharp crag. We had been warned by a couple staying at our hotel about getting too close to the cliffs that bounded the island—they had spent ten summers on Patmos and had heard awful things over the years. I walked into the water until it reached my knees, unsure whether my fever of anticipation had deluded me into suspecting the worst. His head broke the surface in the middle of the bay. He waved me over.

Grilled fish at the taverna. Eggplant and boiled vegetables. We discussed books over a dessert of fries and beer. Last night, Shiv met the Frenchman, Corentin, for dinner at a restaurant about a mile north of us. They hadn't yet spoken about their lives off Patmos and the anonymity of the encounter made him curious. Who was this man with a medium-length cock and lack of recognizable personality outside of his insatiable hunger for ass? They ate humus and salad. Corentin lived in Paris and worked for his family's grocery chain, but otherwise he had no interest in talking about his life in France or in learning any more about Shiv's than what he already knew. Which wasn't much. They talked about the weather and the other islands he had visited since he started coming to Greece as a child. When Shiv pressed him if he had a boyfriend or a partner, he said, "Yes, he was with me the day you and I met." They walked in the dark to Skala, stopped at the hill where they had first fucked, and fucked again among the chickens.

Shiv said, "We should go to Chora tomorrow after the Cave."

"I thought you wanted to wait until the 21st?"

"What day is it?"

Flickers of service.

From: telemachos@xxxxxxxfoundation.gr
To: andrew.durbin@gmail.com
Date: Thu, August 17, 2017 at 5:34 PM
Subject: Alekos

But I couldn't open the body of the message. Was he leaving?

"Nah," Shiv said.

In Greece, he was less anxious than he had been in New York. The frenetic days of running errands across town, seeing friends at bars and poetry readings, scrambling to finish his dissertation were over—for now. He never mentioned the progress he had made toward its final chapters, which might have meant he'd abandoned it but wouldn't say. Nothing bothered him. No rush. This frustrated me at the start of the trip—mostly because I couldn't seem to let go of New York nearly as easily as he had. (I sometimes forget that he's had a year to do so; once we were together again, it was like no time had passed.) New York constructs a mobile version of itself in each of its residents, as demanding as the real one, always insisting I check my phone for service—what, in the middle of nowhere at the end of summer, do I need to look up or read?—or the time. Noon, two-thirty, five, seven-fifteen. Except for degrees of light, the hours were mostly no different from one another. Time waned, and I felt it wane. That was the waiting. But what was I waiting for? Shiv assured me that we had *arrived*, that we were *where we needed to be*.

Alekos, who I was beginning to suspect might have left the island already, would still be in Chora. But what about the emails?

He wants to know if you found the painting yet," Shiv said

After enough retsina, I found his lack of worry contagious. *Yes, yes*, I thought. *He's right; there's no harm in staying put, in taking our time, in enjoying ourselves.* We came to Patmos for more than research, after all. We came to catch up after a year apart.

"He's probably wondering where you are. Can you pass me the bottle?"

"Well, exactly!"

We sat on the balcony, eating feta from a plastic container.

"Let's go out," he said. Seeing my face, "Don't worry. It's almost the 21st."

After midnight, the bars in Skala closed. We searched the streets, failed to find one that might stay open for us, changed into our swim trunks and waded into the sea. The ferry drifts into town every third night, arriving with the huge blast of a horn. One chugged into the dock while we sat in the shallows. More passengers boarded than left. Those who landed piled into taxis and drove, in a neat and winding column of cars, up the mountain to Chora. How long had we been on Patmos? The retsina made the math difficult.

AUGUST 19

A jewelry designer was staying at his husband's family home on the mountain. They had landed a few nights ago, with an entourage of young men from Athens, Paris, and London, mostly old friends and boyfriends they had picked up over the summer. The designer, who I met on a cruising app, told me he was bored and wanted to know if I would like to come to their house for a party. It was late, a cab would be difficult to find, if not impossible, and I didn't have cash. He wrote that he could borrow a Moped and visit me instead, if that was easier. Cell service was limited. Shiv was somewhere with Corentin and said he didn't think he'd be back until morning. I sent the designer my address.

He was handsome, older by five years than his profile had indicated, with a slight scruff on his neck, and eyes weighed down by dark, baggy skin. He and his husband had been moving between islands since early July, from Mykonos to Santorini to Crete, with a few smaller ones between, until they finally reached Patmos. The designer brought cocaine, a bottle of tequila, lube, and condoms in a black Prada satchel, its zipper tied with a silver chain. We sat on the communal porch and watched the wavering penumbra of moonlight embalm the Aegean while he cut lines and told me about his trip, which he had spent with men and some women he didn't know well, in places where he couldn't quite feel at home, while wondering whether his relationship was ending. It was ending, he told me, and he hoped it would end amicably, not with one man leaving in a rage or shutting the other out of their social circle in London. London is a big city full of transient people, but it was important they not damage their shared lives there, even if those lives were increasingly spent apart, he explained. But, again, it was ending and, as an ending, it couldn't be reversed. I wondered if he was lying, or else testing some alternative version of his life that might make him more compelling as a character, as a one-night stand, someone I might sympathize with, even feel sad for, before I sucked his dick.

He wondered what I had done on Patmos and I told him every day had been mostly the same: a quick breakfast, followed by a swim, then slow meals for lunch and dinner, usually consisting of charred meats and cold pitchers of wine. Sometimes Shiv and I would taxi to a faraway beach and read poems or watch men. The designer nodded along. He couldn't take his eyes off the moon except when he needed to mind his hands as he cut the cocaine with a credit card. He finished and said, "Voila." He did a line, then I did a line. Our pace of conversation moved at a faster clip as he opened the tequila and poured us shots. I told him I was on Patmos to search for a painting—I lied and said it was of an old friend, someone who had passed away—but I wasn't sure I would find what I was looking for, it might even be lost. Or didn't exist.

The designer understood. Rare but famous jewelry was often difficult to recover since centuries of total war in Europe had jeopardized countless personal collections and institutions. He had known collectors who traveled the world in search of one piece, a necklace or bracelet or ring, only to find that each person who supposedly owned it was either dead and their belongings dispersed or wrong about what they had. "These things happen," he said. "I met my husband while on a trip to find a piece. He was living in Paris and had inherited a necklace from his grandmother—a very beautiful Prussian object—a sapphire pendant. I loved him immediately."

He didn't have a picture of the pendant. They had sold it to an Austrian collector soon after they met, and now it's housed in the Kunsthistorisches Museum in Vienna. The first tingle of the drug zipped up my spine. The designer's face pulsed in the moonlight, his personality haloed by my sympathy for his impending loss. Maybe. Even if the dilemma were made up, it still nagged at me: that he needed a thing—some rich loveless husband on the mountain—to attract my attention. I considered both possibilities, real husband and false, as I brought my nose to the table to snort another line. Both appeared in my mind as converging realities that shed their contradictions. Nameless feeling.

Either you search or move on, accept the painting as lost, out of reach, or otherwise destroyed. Or—the likeliest—that it never was, and the whole thing is an elaborate fiction concocted by a writer in his last days. The answer might lie in Guibert's refusal to describe the painting in the first place. Perhaps he never went to Corfu, never met Tsarouchis, and the episode was as pretend as those in *Paradise*. I buzzed with the possibility of my biography-through-the-periphery being shaped not by the real things Guibert left behind—the stories of friends and lovers and artists he knew—but by invented objects, the things-that-never-were-and-never-could-have-been. Those shards of a life possessed, in their unreality, a kind of fantastic gravity, a force—and control—that shaped real life from their place at the center of imagination. The portrait. Corfu. Patmos. The Greek painter and his island were based on other people and other places, their names lost to me. They were fiction, and only a fiction could rescue life from banality. As such, Guibert (and my biography) required fantasy, too, and character, like friends in Athens who know of islands where paintings are said to lurk behind the walls of ancient cities. I didn't necessarily need a real painting, though a real painting would help.

I felt the designer's hand slide up my thigh, into my shorts. My breathing became shallow.

"Can I kiss you?" he asked.

I nodded. His lips tasted of chemicals. He slid his forefinger through the netting of my swim trunks and under my balls.

"Is this all right?"

My tongue struggled to find its way as we kissed, seeking farther into his throat, though I wasn't sure what I wanted from his mouth except more of it, for it to swallow me as I tried to swallow him.

We moved to my room. His pants were held together by an elaborate set of folds buttoned across the crotch, which he struggled to undo, especially since he was so drunk and high. I liked that he had lied to me about his age, that he was closer to forty than thirty-five. His belly showed slack, but so did mine. We lay in bed and he pawed at my chest. His small cock nested in a tuft of pubic hair, curling slightly to the right. I held it as we kissed. I wasn't the husband, his mind was elsewhere, the coke had left him cold. He said, "I don't think I'm feeling this. I'm out of it."

"That's fine." I wondered if I had done something wrong or if he thought I was unattractive. The days on the island, in a small room without a mirror, had warped my self-image. I no longer knew what I looked like, what anyone but Shiv thought of me.

"Do you mind if I sleep a little?"

"No, I think you should go."

"Really? We can try again in the morning. I don't feel like driving to my place."

"I'd prefer for you to leave. It's too hot."

"Frustrating."

"I've had a long day and I need to sleep. I can't with someone else in a bed this small."

It creaked in agreement beneath us.

"I'm not going to get any sleep up there either. They'll be awake all night."

"I'm sorry," I said. I didn't quite mean it. He had a big house, with plenty of rooms. He would make do.

"I thought you'd be nicer," he said, standing up to collect his clothes. What had given him that impression? How had I been especially cruel? He struggled with the buttons on his pants, eventually gave up and tied two swathes of fabric into a loose knot that held tight to his waist. I handed him his satchel and he took it with an irritated sigh.

"It was nice to meet you," I said and followed him out to the courtyard.

He turned on the stair that led to the lot where he had parked. His lips moved slightly. The words, whatever he might have thought to say, didn't come. I watched him knock the kickstand in place with his Italian boot and putter off, toward Chora.

AUGUST 20

Shiv arrived at our place early in the morning and went to town for coffee. A sign on the docks, where he sipped espresso and watched the boats drift to sea, advertised a ferry service to Lipsi with several returns throughout the day. On the 23rd, the island will celebrate its annual religious festival, one of the most important in the East Aegean, dedicated to the image of the Virgin Mary cradling Christ on the cross. The church places dry sprigs of lily in the picture's glass frame—an homage to a woman who Mary visited while she was praying in a small chapel in the countryside. "Something very special to see," the ferryman said. A parade will carry the icon through town, accompanied by a long evening feast, which everyone is free to attend, even two Americans staying on Patmos. "Better to go a few days early, before the festival, though, if you're more interested in beaches," he told Shiv. "There is one very good spot, at the far end of the island, where Homer is said to have shacked up with a woman who inspired his portrait of Calypso in the *Odyssey*. The icon will be at the church, too. Go now and, if you like it enough, return on the 23rd. A quick trip, not very expensive." Shiv bought two tickets and we left, around ten this morning, for Lipsi.

We were the only tourists on the boat. Elderly Greek men and women, their faces sunken and leathery, stared at us from under covered benches on the main deck when we boarded, tracking our movements closely. They were more attentive than anyone we had met on Patmos so far; the other islanders mostly ignored the non-Greeks when we passed them on the street or in tavernas. I wondered if we might have violated some unspoken rule about crossing from Patmos to Lipsi on a Sunday. The ferryman took our tickets without saying a word.

Other than the custom against nudity, which wasn't enforced by any lifeguards or police, nothing about life on the island had, so far, suggested the underlying conservatism I immediately recognized in the faces on the ferry, with their mistrusting eyes. These people, in their best suits and dresses, belonged to another island than the Patmos we had seen so far, one independent of the tourist circuit Shiv and I had followed for the past week. Shiv said, "Let's sit on the roof. This feels weird." We found a bench on the second level, in front of a younger crowd who tolerated the bright sunshine out of respect for the elders, mostly handsome young men who sat together in small groups. I could feel their eyes on the back of my head, too. "They're staring at me," Shiv clarified.

The ferry gained speed once we cleared the wake of the sailboats idling near Skala. Shiv's suntan lotion scented the air around us, a faintly lemony American brand we both liked. Behind us, the young men had already fallen asleep, their low-cut shorts bunched around their crotches to reveal heavily tanned thighs. I kept turning to stare at their huge, hairy legs stretched along the white plastic benches. They were hefty and beautiful. Shiv sat quietly, his mind on the island coming into view.

If Homer had lived on Lipsi, he would have seen exactly what we saw—a jagged lump of sand on the horizon. In a funny way, the thought of him sailing by ancient skiff to the same barren-looking island to which we were now headed broke the feeling of anticipation that had gripped me for days. We were pursuing a clear-cut path, one taken for thousands of years by thousands of people whose names and lives couldn't be known; who had traveled from faraway places to write poetry or to find a painting of someone they never knew but somehow loved. The sea shushed rhythmically against the side of the boat as we slowed. It had a voice, and it didn't. Shiv was still bothered by the looks the other passengers had given us when we boarded, but I'd already forgotten them—they were melded with the centuries as one transhistorical face. A haggard face, the same face as that of the first people who settled this part of the world, before the invention of writing (which happened twice in the Aegean, with a long illiterate dark age between the two alphabets developed at the dawn of history) and through the Greek civilizations that had struggled and collapsed for generations until, finally, they mustered the technology to not only live, but to record that they had lived—out here, among olive groves and fig trees and goats and beaches and tavernas without refrigeration and hotels without internet. My forehead burned in the sun. Those meaty thighs caught the heat and the light as the men snoozed.

It was strange that we hadn't tested Patmos by stripping naked in the daylight and seeing, finally, what breaking its one rule might reveal about the island. We had thoughtlessly conceded to the ambiguous authority of the Citadel, even when we went swimming on the empty beaches, where no one would have protested because no one was around to complain about our bare asses. Maybe Lipsi would be different: its church was smaller and had no mountain from which it might spy on us. On Patmos, the huge and omnipresent Citadel had an almost gravitational moral force; it exerted its control on the island through a constellation of cab drivers and taverna owners and the passive acceptance of tourists, assuring a way of life would always be preserved—one without many gay men, fewer young people than we had expected, and no people of color except Shiv. Being naked, and not furtively fucking, is only a tiny revolt, the smallest of any supposedly radical gesture we might muster against the Citadel, but I wasn't sure why I hadn't attempted it yet—at least until I saw the sullen Greeks on the boat, for whom this rule presumably matters a great deal. I imagined the scene once we tried it, the elderly islanders rising up from nowhere, from under the pebbles and out of the trees, to wrap us in our clothes and towels or else drag us into the sea. Where had we even heard that nudity was banned? The cab driver? Who else? Perhaps the rule originated with us and was no more than projection. Elsewhere in the Aegean nudity is common, or so Corentin said. "Then why is he here?" I asked. Shiv had no clue.

How to describe the conditions of island life that presupposed our visit: those who were born here, and those who were not. Even the idea of "island life," a phrase that suggests an undergirding set of rules and customs, only came to me on the boat, after Patmos had diminished into the distance. Its apartness finally struck me as we bounced on the waves.

An unwritten law built up over millennia, which can only be understood through its violation.

An old Greek word, *autochthonous*, meaning "born of the soil."

We should have swum naked.

The soft, rocky dirt of the hills ran down to the shore. Octopuses hung from ropes across Lipsi Town's main square, between houses and restaurants, dripping rosaries of rubbery purple flesh. Otherwise, the buildings were few, low, and squat, with the exception of the church, which stood on a small hill above the town. A large crowd had gathered either to greet or board our boat; among them, about a dozen soldiers. Three Army Jeeps were parked in a nearby lot. We mimicked the others and waved to the islanders. Everyone but the soldiers waved back.

"We shouldn't have come," I said. The soldiers trained their eyes on the top deck, where we stood.

Shiv, who had been silent since we arrived at the dock, nodded, "Yeah, maybe. It's smaller than I thought."

"What's with the soldiers?"

"That's what I was thinking."

We were the last to disembark and most of the passengers had already dispersed. The soldiers stepped forward and I realized, too late, that they had not been waiting to board: they had been waiting for us. Three grabbed Shiv and another soldier, he must have been eighteen, with fair hair and a slanted mouth, moved me to the side.

"What's going on?" Shiv shouted.

The soldiers escorted him to their Jeeps. A few townsfolk watched us from the porch of a grocery. None stepped forward to ask what was happening to us, if we needed help translating between Greek and English. I recognized in their flat expressions the even keel of a satisfied patience, that what they had been waiting for while we clipped between the islands had finally come about. Someone on the boat must have radioed ahead.

"Can you tell me what's happening?" I asked the soldier.

He shook his head.

"What did we do?"

"We need to see your passport. Are you staying on Lipsi? Where did you find this man?"

"He's my friend. We came over from Patmos. I left my passport at the hotel. I have my wallet. Here." I performed reaching into my bathing-suit pocket—slowly, shakily, so as not to alarm him. He shook his head again. He didn't want my wallet.

I could see Shiv gesturing wildly to his captors. Some kicked dirt while they listened to him, dragging on their hand-rolled cigarettes. The sound of his nervous voice carried in the air, but I couldn't make out what he was saying.

"How long have you been on Patmos? Look at me. Look at *me*."

"Since the 15th. We're visiting from New York."

"*Both* of you?"

"Yes. We're traveling together. All of our stuff is on Patmos. Here—here's my American ID."

He considered it, then handed it over, "Wait."

The soldiers huddled amongst themselves. Their interest in the contents of Shiv's wallet grew. They inspected his debit and credit cards, brought his New York ID up to the light, as if considering whether it might be fake. Smiles and laughter broke out after they concluded what to do with him. Shiv nodded enthusiastically, answered more of their questions, and waited for the soldiers to hand over his wallet. Their commanding officer tapped it against his hand as he lectured Shiv, his eyes narrowing as he did so, then returned it after flipping through its contents once more. Shiv was free to go.

The unit drove off in their Jeeps toward the countryside, cutting past the townspeople and stragglers from our boat who had waited to see what the soldiers might do to us, their faces as menacing as when we had crossed the water. Otherwise, the town was empty, the restaurants closed. When we cleared the main street, Shiv turned left, saying nothing, onto a road lined with bent fig trees that ran to the far end of the island. He said, "They thought you were sneaking me into Europe. I don't want to talk about it. They told me how to get to the beach. We should take the next boat to Patmos. It's in three hours."

Children played with ducks in the shallow water. The sand was a mixture of colorful pebbles. A few families—all Greek—picnicked under a large yew, sometimes breaking into song and games. One father roasted sausage on a makeshift grill and offered us a plate of links and roasted peppers. Shiv politely declined, though we hadn't eaten all day. The old taverna was closed for the sabbath. We watched the waves and tried to imagine the Homeric similes they might have inspired, but neither of us had read the *Iliad* or the *Odyssey* in years. This angry island. We invented our own metaphors for the morning

99

and afternoon, then fell silent until it was time to sail to Patmos, like oxen driving into salted earth.

AUGUST 21

The path to the Cave begins at the south end of Skala, past ice cream parlors and creperies, where tourists cluster in long, disorganized lines. Once through the outskirts of town, the houses taper off, the creperies give way to abandoned buildings, a few out-of-place mansions, and the streets converge into a rough trail, its incline more pronounced with every step. With Skala behind us, we crossed a modern road that spirals around the mountain and continued deeper into patchy forest.

In Skala, the architecture is mostly new, with ancient or seemingly ancient buildings sitting uneasily among the jewelry shops and restaurants. I had no idea how old anything was. Most of the town must date to sometime in the mid-20th century, with its post-war simplicity of precision-cut walls and windows of pristine glass. No soft, hand-sculpted edges. Old parts of town, like the stony outcrop where John rid himself of the Devil or the font where he baptized ancient Patmos, are unprotected by fences or high walls; the font sits by the side of the road that loops the island's coast, dusty from the passing cars and buses. I had visited the font most mornings and evenings of my stay so far— it's a few steps from the nearest café—and I hadn't once seen anyone else pay homage to the basin, not even the priests from Chora. These old places sit quietly in their corners, or else hide in plain sight, humbled by having been forgotten by everyone.

Shiv said, "I should have brought more water. It's so fucking hot today." We finished our bottles as soon as we left Skala. It wasn't a very long walk up to the Cave—only half an hour, but a late-summer heatwave had fallen upon the island, and we had chosen to trek at the high point of the swelter.

When would the eclipse begin back home? Likely, it already had. Whether our visit to the Cave of the Apocalypse would conjunct with the event in North America no longer mattered. It seemed as if I had left New York long ago (the week might have been a year or more) and whatever the Cave's potential magic, was now irrelevant, replaced in our minds with the unthinking need to check a box before we left the island. We hardly spoke on the hike.

I kept seeing Guibert. He stepped behind a large tree in the middle of an arid patch of mountain then faded in the shimmer of air. Later, I found him sitting on a rock in the woods among his friends, including a young Christine and Thierry. He smiled at me before turning to them. Or, no, to Jayne. He looked less like the photographs of him than he did Julien, with Julien's long hair hanging over his narrow face, slightly tanned from sunbathing all summer on my roof. Both men have small, intensely bright eyes. Julien's lips are bigger but, on the path up to the Cave, his lips were Guibert's. And then he was gone.

I texted Julien, during a surprise moment of service as we ascended the mountain, "Sorry, I didn't respond to you last week. No excuse. Did you go home to see the eclipse?"

He had said before I left that he would drive to his parents' house in Virginia, where the view would be best owing to the sun's curved trajectory over the continent.

New York is slightly out of range.

From our vantage on the side of the mountain, the Aegean surrounded the islands like a blue pavement. Within the ocean, eddies, underwater cyclones, a flow between merging bodies of water—that is Greek time. It rushes under, circles, slows down, flows in smaller and larger movements. Sometimes, I swam very fast within it; at other times, I went nowhere at all.

Julien replied, "I did. I sort of got it?"

His sent a photo of the eclipse but it wouldn't load. I could imagine it all the same. The bright disk of the sun would be much smaller than expected, owing to the strange distance the iPhone camera adds between the picture-taker and their subjects. Its evacuated center: the circle of moon crossing between the sun and the Earth. The sky was another matter. It should be dark, but perhaps that wouldn't come through on the phone, which tends to improve upon its users' skills by brightening the image.

"It won't load, but I'll see it later. We're almost to the Cave of Apocalypse. I've missed you."

"Send me pictures later. And you'll have to tell me if you found the painting. I've missed you too."

"Up here," Shiv said. "There." A sign marking the way to the Cave was posted a few feet ahead. It indicated that a European Union commission for the preservation of historic sites in Europe, in collaboration with UNESCO, maintained the site on behalf of the people of Patmos. We climbed still farther into a stone grotto filled with kittens sunbathing on a pile of dry leaves. A white building housed a newish museum at the front of the Cave, but its door was locked and a sign reported that the religious site was only open on Sundays, Tuesdays, and Thursdays.

"What day is it?" I asked.

"Monday."

"I feel dumb," Shiv said, reaching down to pick up a kitten lying near the locked door.

"Me too."

"We shouldn't."

"Who could have known?"

"Someone with access to the internet."

"The kiosk guy who gave us the map."

"Yeah, him."

"Well…Chora?"

"Time to find your painting."

We spent forty minutes searching Chora's streets for the bar, in a maze of chalk-white walls and shuttered windows, until we found the brown door with a sign that read Astivi in English, though we didn't know how many turns we had taken from the town's entrance, and I'm not sure we could have located it again. It was sometime after seven. Greeks and tourists were beginning to make their way inside for cocktail hour. We were still an hour from sunset, but the light had obtained its terrific sharpness that usually occurs toward end of day. When we arrived at the bar's roof, we could see clear to

Samos, with its huge peak—the tallest in the Aegean—catching the sun. There were several couples occupying tables across the roof. Most were Western Europeans, though some spoke Greek. Waiters in disheveled blue uniforms, rather than starched white, moved slowly between tables, without any sense of urgency, which was the standard for restaurants not only on this island, but throughout the entire country, where no dinner takes less than three hours. Even when you've finished every dish and you couldn't possibly have more of the endless small plates provided for free by generous restaurants in order to keep you from leaving, waiters find ways to prolong your meal with complimentary dessert liqueurs. No table at Astivi had received any food yet; instead, patrons sat drinking chilled red wine and wet martinis.

"Him," Shiv pointed out. "The guy in the corner." At the far end, an older man sat reading a book with a purple cover, its Greek title embossed in gold. His hair was gray, thick, and rose up from his widow's peak into a modest plume. He had circular glasses, behind which his blue eyes focused intently on the book. He didn't have a cocktail, only a bottle of sparkling water.

He was different than I had imagined him, though we both knew he was Alekos. I had pictured a more rugged, homely man, not this handsome, thin figure, whose features combined the cold, wrinkled austerity of Samuel Beckett with the middle-European elegance of someone like Balthus—another famous painter featured in *The Man in the Red Hat*. In fact, Alekos, sitting at his corner table, was not simply the owner of a portrait of Guibert, he *was* Balthus—or, at least, an apparition of Balthus. Still alive, even though he had died sixteen years ago, at the turn of the century.

In 1984 Guibert glimpsed Balthus at the Cannes Film Festival and managed to interview him for *Le Monde*. Their conversation was brief but compelling enough to remain on Guibert's mind long after he had turned in final copy. Two years later, he dialed the painter before a trip to Switzerland; Balthus was then living in Lausanne, and Guibert wanted to see if he could pay him a visit. He agreed. "Balthus said he was wanting to paint a nude that would not be naked," Guibert writes of his afternoon at the painter's home, "or else a nude that would be nothing but a nude, a nude that would be at one and the same time nothing and the idea of a nude, a sublime nude, without sex appeal, an absolutely discarnate nude."

Guibert identifies the painting as *Nude with Crow*, a title which he must have invented for Balthus's 1986 work *Large Composition with Crow*. This slight revision is telling, since it suggests that either Guibert made up the painting *Nude with Crow*, and he isn't referring to *Large Composition with Crow*, or else he forgot a key feature: it contains not one nude, but two. A woman lies on a bed; beside her, a tiny man holds a table or footstool with his back facing the viewer. The woman has an expression of crazed glee—she is unlike so many of Balthus's paintings of reclining women—and raises her hand to gesture toward the crow.

Guibert and Balthus are in agreement on the presence of the bird, but Guibert doesn't seem to realize the painter was being quite literal in his desire to paint a "discarnate nude." In *Large Composition with Crow*, Balthus presents two tropes: in the man, the emphasis is placed on the faceless classicism of his muscular form, as in many paintings of male bathers that were popular in the 19th century, though, in a slight twist on the theme, he is strangely small, no bigger than the footstool he holds. In the woman, Balthus portrays the even-more famous trope of the Odalisque, only she appears maddened by the absurd scenario she has awoken to and not at peace in a warm bed attended by servants (or slaves). Between them and the crow, there is a black wall, the work's true nude: lacking shape, unadorned, a blank—it is the nude that would be "at one and the same time nothing." Crow, man, and woman seem, at first, to be looking at one another, but I read them as beckoning my attention to the "discarnate" figure Balthus told Guibert he wished to paint, the invisible person—or thing—the world is dragging into existence, but which never materializes: the painting's true subject. It is Guibert, or Time, or Nowhere, or Patmos, or Shiv, or Julien, or Heyer, or Alekos, or Fiction, or Samos, or the Crisis, or an Ending.

"Are you Alekos?" I asked the man.

He nodded. "You must be the friend of Telemachos. Mr. Andrew, no? He told me you would be coming, but I thought it would be days ago and I feared I had missed you."

Shiv apologized, "I'm sorry. We were delayed."

"All the same," Alekos said. "Sit."

We took a seat at his table.

"I am afraid I have bad news," he started. "I told Telemachos to write to you—I would have done so myself, but I didn't have your e-mail address. He was not quite right in telling you that I had this painting you are searching for, the one of Hervé."

"OK," I said. "I see."

"It is true that I was friends with Yannis and Hervé, but I did not know Hervé through Yannis. He knew an acquaintance of mine in Paris, a journalist with whom he was lovers for some time. The connection is funny, even to me, and not worth getting into here. But what matters for you is that I don't have any painting of him, no, no, and I am sorry you have come all this way thinking I do. I have a Yannis painting of two young Greek men from Arta, near Corfu. I am happy to show you—and you will see immediately it is not Hervé. It is very small, a gift."

A waiter approached us with a menu. "You'll have a drink?" Alekos asked. "My treat."

The small Tsarouchis painting hung in a blue room above a wooden table stacked with books in English and French. The boys from Arta sat on a rock, or a few brush strokes that approximated a rock. One's hairy legs were crossed, his right arm resting on a knee. The other held a few flowers out to his friend. They both wore white shorts, the folds of which were more meticulously rendered

114

than any other part of the painting. The figures themselves were provisional, with the lines demarcating them from the landscape thin, sometimes incomplete. The boys' thighs and elbows joined rocks, their heads the sky. Their impassive expressions were made using the fewest possible lines—single strokes for the mouths, two ovular dots for eyes, light eyebrows. Their skin was the color of Patmos, or Arta. Born of the soil, still soil. I don't know what either of us had expected of it, but in its smallness, in its spartan lines and monotone of thick brown and sandy-colored paint, in its scene of two boys who were by now middle-aged men living somewhere in Greece, in their finely muscular figures that would have been antithetical to the thinner and sickly Guibert who Tsarouchis supposedly painted in Corfu, the picture was perfect. More perfect than Guibert's portrait would have been had we found it. Shiv and I stood in the room, at the end of summer, in another century that bore little resemblance to the one that had produced this painting. It was cut from a supreme air and landscape, and it

115

allowed us a glimpse of a past we would never access, which had been closed off by forces that preceded us and could never be undone. Everything that had been part of that world, including the missing portrait of Guibert, belonged to the past completely, and would remain there forever, just out of reach. These boys: we had seen men like them countless times on the island. We had seen them on the beaches at Psili Ammos and even as waiters at Astivi. They were everywhere and nowhere at once; we had spoken to them, watched them, listened to their voices. Shiv had even fucked one. They were on Lipsi too. Guibert was among them and so were we.

AUGUST 22

Psili Ammos, again. The beach was emptier. Summer was nearly over, everyone had to go home, to work and to school, to France and Germany and the United Kingdom and New York City. A donkey tied to an ancient tree moaned in the shade. It jerked at its rope, clanging a bell for water. No one bothered. Its owners, the family who ran the taverna, played cards under the awning attached to the kitchen and listened to sports radio. I watched the children eat salty fries and dig their feet into sand. The waves grew rougher and Shiv ran headlong into the sea.

"The weather here," Guibert wrote in his diaries, "almost terrifying, between loss and abundance."

ACKNOWLEDGMENTS

In 2018, *Tinted Window* published a short version of this novella in their inaugural issue, which was devoted to the work of Hervé Guibert. Thank you to Stephen Motika of Nightboat Books for his friendship and for nudging me to finish what I had left undone. I'm also grateful, as ever, to Steven Zultanski for his encouragement and close reading.

You can support refugees in the Mediterranean and elsewhere by volunteering or donating to the International Rescue Committee at rescue.org.

ANDREW DURBIN is the author of several books, including *MacArthur Park* (2017), which was a finalist for the 2018 Believer Book Award. He is the editor of *frieze* magazine and lives in London.

NIGHTBOAT BOOKS

Nightboat Books, a nonprofit organization, seeks to develop audiences for writers whose work resists convention and transcends boundaries. We publish books rich with poignancy, intelligence, and risk. Please visit nightboat.org to learn about our titles and how you can support our future publications.

The following individuals have supported the publication of this book. We thank them for their generosity and commitment to the mission of Nightboat Books:

Kazim Ali
Anonymous
Jean C. Ballantyne
Photios Giovanis
Amanda Greenberger
Elizabeth Motika
Benjamin Taylor
Peter Waldor
Jerrie Whitfield & Richard Motika

In addition, this book has been made possible, in part, by grants from the New York City Department of Cultural Affairs in partnership with the City Council and the New York State Council on the Arts Literature Program.